Happy Halloween!

Grosset & Dunlap

Based upon the animated series *Max & Ruby*
A Nelvana Limited production © 2002–2003.

Max & Ruby™ and © Rosemary Wells. NELVANA™ Nelvana Limited. CORUS™ Corus Entertainment Inc. All Rights Reserved.
Used under license by Penguin Young Readers Group. Published in 2008 by Grosset & Dunlap, a division of Penguin Young Readers Group,
345 Hudson Street, New York, New York 10014. GROSSET & DUNLAP is a trademark of Penguin Group (USA) Inc. Printed in the U.S.A.

Library of Congress Control Number: 2007040008

ISBN 978-0-448-44863-3   10 9 8

It was Halloween.

"Max, where are you?" asked Max's sister, Ruby. "It's time to go trick-or-treating!"

"Boo!" said Max as he jumped out of the wardrobe.
"That didn't scare me, Max," said Ruby.

Ruby answered the telephone.
Max sent a rubber spider down on a string.
"Boo!" said Max.
"That didn't scare me one bit, Max," said Ruby.

Ruby opened up her trick-or-treating basket.

Out popped some rubber worms.

"Boo!" said Max.

"Oh silly," said Ruby. "I'm not scared!"

**Suddenly Max disappeared.
"Where's Max?" asked Ruby.**

Ruby was sure she knew where Max went.

"Boo!" said Max as he jumped out of the closet.

"I knew you were in there, Max!" said Ruby.

Max put spiders in Ruby's shoes.
"Boo!" said Max.
"It's impossible to scare me, Max!"
said Ruby.

"Oops!" said Ruby. "I've lost my fairy wand. Let me go find it, Max!"

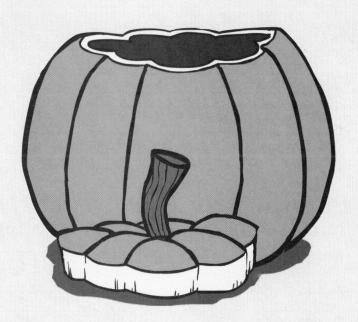

Max followed Ruby to her room.
"Boo!" said Max.
But Ruby wasn't there.

Max went downstairs looking for Ruby. It was dark.

"Boo!" said Max.

But Ruby wasn't there. Where could she be?

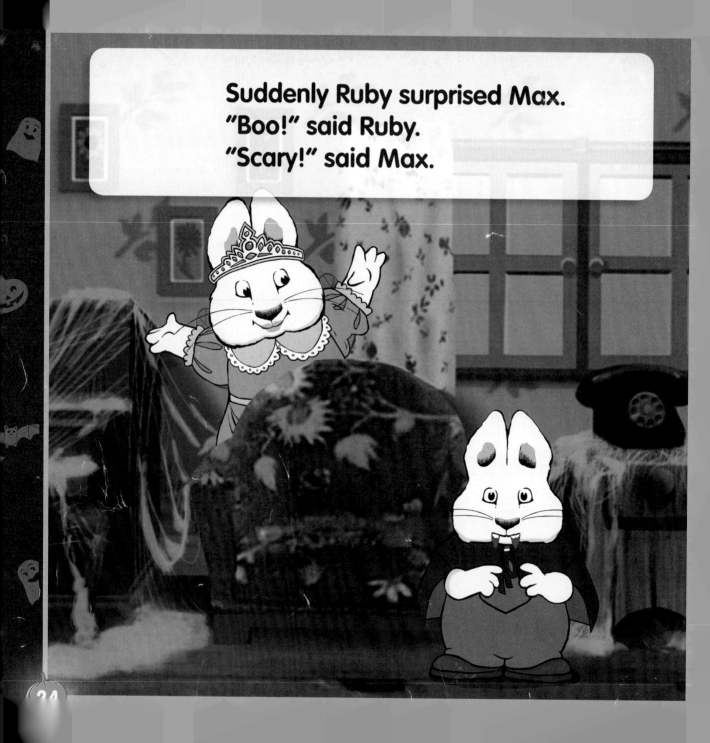

Suddenly Ruby surprised Max.
"Boo!" said Ruby.
"Scary!" said Max.